To Levi and Nero - J.C.

# tiger tales

5 River Road, Suite 128, Wilton, CT 06897
Published in the United States 2018
Originally published in Great Britain 2018
by Little Tiger Press
Text and illustrations copyright © 2018 Jane Chapman
Visit Jane Chapman at www.ChapmanandWarnes.com
ISBN-13: 978-1-68010-084-6
ISBN-10: 1-68010-084-X
Printed in China
LTP/1400/1991/0817

For more insight and activities,
visit us at www.tigertalesbooks.com

# With your Paw in Mine

by Jane Chapman

tiger tales

From the moment she was born,
Miki loved to snuggle on Mama's tufty tummy.
"Mama, you are the softest pillow in the
WHOLE ocean!" she sighed happily.

All around them was cold sea and empty sky,
but Miki felt safe as the waves gently rocked her.

"Time for a swimming lesson!" smiled Mama.
"Let's fluff you up so you'll float when the big waves come."

Mama pawed Miki's fur until she was as puffy
as a pompom! Miki couldn't help wiggling.
"That TICKLES!" she giggled.

"Come on then, fuzzy," laughed Mama,
sliding her into the water.
"Put your paws in mine and

kick those feet!"

When it was lunchtime,
Mama rolled her pup over
and over in the seaweed until
only Miki's paws stuck out.

"Roly poly, roly poly!" sang Mama.
"This will keep you from drifting away
while I look for something to eat."
She gave Miki a kiss, then flicked
her tail and dove into the ocean.

Miki was snug in the kelp fronds, but she missed Mama.

Nearby was another furry bundle just like her.
*I wonder if that's an otter?* Miki thought,
paddling over to see.

"Er . . . hello!" she smiled shyly.

"I'm Miki. What's your name?"

"I'm Amak," replied the other bundle.

"I'm waiting for my mama;
she's gone hunting."

"Me, too!" said Miki. "Waiting is lonely, isn't it?"
Amak nodded, so Miki paddled a little closer.

"Let's wait for our mamas together," she suggested bravely.
"We could hold paws, too . . . if you like."

Amak smiled. "I'd like that," he said.

From then on, Miki and Amak always stayed close together while their mamas went hunting.

Miki taught Amak how to float upside-down and admire the feathery forest below.

"Wow! Look, Miki!" called Amak, as turtles sped through the water beneath them.

At night, after fluffing up their fur,
the mamas and babies cuddled together.

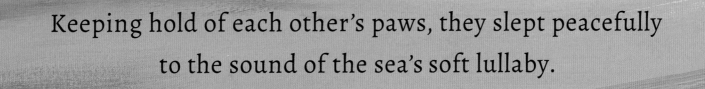

Keeping hold of each other's paws, they slept peacefully
to the sound of the sea's soft lullaby.

One morning, while Miki and Amak were
splish-splashing and their mamas were away
hunting, the sky began to darken.

"Where did the sun go?" asked Miki.
"And what happened to the sea?"
The blue-green waves had turned black
and white, and rain was falling all around.

"I don't like this, Miki," whispered Amak. "I'm scared!"
Miki was scared, too. She wanted Mama.

Suddenly, a huge wave crashed and —SNAP!—
the seaweed tore beneath them!
Miki and Amak were pulled apart
in a whirl of sea, spray, and sky.

"Amak! Amak, grab my paw!"
cried Miki above the wind.

Amak reached out, stretching
as far as he could . . .

. . . until the two pups were paw in paw on the
rumbling, tumbling tide.
"I'm glad you're here!" shouted Miki.
"I feel safer with you!"

But then they heard other voices —
babies and mamas calling out over the water.

"Help!"

"This way!"

"Grab my paw!"

Miki and Amak were joined by more and more
otters, all reaching out to grab on to one another.

The wind blew and the waves crashed, but the raft of otters clung tightly together as the storm raged on.

And then, over the howling wind, Miki heard her favorite voice in all the ocean calling her name.
"Mama!" she called back.

Mama swung Miki up for a snuggle.
"What a storm!" she whispered.

"I missed you, Mama," sniffled Miki.
"But Amak and I took care of each other!"

Mama smiled down at her brave pup, cuddling her tight
until the winds dropped, the waves softened, and the
blue-green ocean was calm once more.

"We all need someone's paw to hold when the big waves come," smiled Mama.

"Well, I have your paw, and Amak's paw . . . and the paws of all our new friends," laughed Miki.

"We'll always have each other!"